RAINBOW

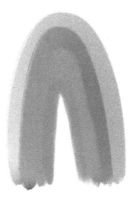

RAINBOW

A NOVELLA

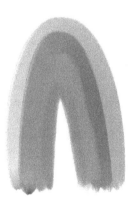

VERDE ARZU

RAINBOW EDITIONS | SACRAMENTO

Published in the United States by Rainbow Editions, in 2019.

First Printing.

Rainbow is a work of fiction. Names, characters, places, and incidents are the product of the author's imagination or are used fictitiously. Any resemblance to actual persons, living or dead, events, or locales is entirely coincidental.

www.verdearzu.com

Cover Illustration by Tara Mixon

Printed and bound in the United States of America.

I dedicate this book to all the Black Women in my life.
You are God's manifestation on earth.
Your power, words of wisdom, encouragement,
and belief in me are reasons why I am able to do this.

CONTENTS

HEART RACING,

PALMS SWEATY

CHAPTER ONE
pregame

MELONY AND I had chemistry from the beginning. I met her on a student union–organized trip to Washington, D.C., in celebration of the tenth anniversary of the Million Man March. Our school's Black Student Union had organized the whole thing: a free trip from Nashville to D.C. They urged everyone who could to join. I sat a few rows from the front of the bus and watched the students pile on. I was glad to have a window seat, and looking forward to the time I would have to just think, relax, and prepare myself for what I imagined was going to be a weekend filled with sadness and anger, but also pride and empowerment.

I was also ecstatic to be seeing one of my favorite artists, Erykah Badu, live. Badu's rich neo-soul sound had been a staple of my childhood. I loved her unique style, how she exuded confidence, her carefree spirit. Although I didn't understand everything she sang about, she was beautiful and alluring, even to my young eyes. My aunt admired her; in fact she'd gone from wearing her hair permed straight to cutting it all off, piercing her nose like Tupac, and wearing headwraps. She was a huge fan, and as a consequence, I became one too.

My headphones crossed my straight-to-the-back cornrows and I bobbed my head to the powerful lyrics and blaring music as I stared out the window—until the smell of her floral scent and the weight of her body falling into the seat next to me pulled my head in her direction. Her eyes were soft. Her hazelnut skin was smooth. Her short, wavy hair was pushed back by a multi-colored headband.

I watched her full lips mouth *Hello*. I smiled and quickly removed my headphones to return her greeting.

"You play for the girls' basketball team, right?" she asked boldly, foregoing the standard introduction.

"Y-yeah, I do." I was startled she recognized me: a third-string point guard who played limited minutes. "You must be a big fan of the team," I ribbed, tickled inside that she knew who I was.

"Something like that," she smiled nodding her head in agreement. "Taylor M. Dawson. Point guard, number twenty-three, like Mike. Averaging about four minutes per game, two points, two assists, zero steals, and one rebound."

I stared at her, bug-eyed.

"I'm Melony." She smiled and pulled her headphones from her bag as she tucked the earbuds into her ears. I watched, still mesmerized, while she searched her music for the right song, then rested her head against her seat and closed her eyes. The desire to press my nose against her neck and inhale came over me. I shook the idea away swiftly, but I was still pulled in. Her smell, her round brown eyes; she had my heart beating like I'd climbed a steep hill. *Fan of the team*, I chuckled to myself. She was definitely a fan of the team if she knew *my* stats by heart. I put my headphones back up, feeling more than a little pride.

As the bus pulled away from campus, Reggie Anderson, one of our school's newest and most vocal BSU members, stood up in the middle of the bus to address everyone.

"First, I just wanna say thank you all for taking the time out to join the BSU on this trip to unite with other like-minded brothers and sisters as we commemorate the tenth anniversary of the Million Man March!" She paused for the hoots and applause. "You could be anywhere else right now, but you understand the importance of this moment, the significance of gathering together in solidarity for the cause of justice, equality, and economic freedom. And I couldn't feel any more happy and blessed to be here with you!"

Another round of cheers filled the bus.

"Isn't she like, a freshman?" Melony frowned. "I mean, she just got here and she acting like she got some seniority," she scoffed.

"Yeah, but I heard she's like twenty-something," I replied, cringing to be brought in on the gossip about the new freshman, who everyone said acted like she thought she was Angela Davis. She was pretty close as far as I was concerned, except for the upkeep of her Afro, which looked more like Don King's than Angela Davis's.

"Oh, so since she old enough to be a senior we gon' go ahead and give her the respect like she one? I guess *so*," she shrugged her shoulders and pursed her lips.

"Why not? I heard she put this trip together almost single-handedly. She's got my respect."

Melony turned and looked at me. "That easy, huh? We'll see," she said.

I swallowed hard and turned back to listen to Reggie. Everyone seemed edgy; only two months prior, Hurricane Katrina had torn through the Gulf Coast, and the people of New Orleans—especially those who lived in the Lower Ninth Ward—had been devestated the most. I listened as Reggie described how Louis Farrakhan believed the city had destroyed the levees on purpose to keep the flooding from destroying the affluent, predominantly White neighborhoods. People from the Lower Ninth had been reporting what sounded like explosions right before the flooding happened. Regardless of what anyone believed, the nation's response to its own desperate citizens—citizens who were fighting for survival—was inexcusable to say the least. Nearly two thousand people died thanks to the country's lethargic response.

Now the Lower Ninth Ward looked like a Third World country in the images on television. Houses were demolished, and those that were still standing looked as if no one had ever lived in them. Spray-painted obituaries were sprawled across homes: the only testament to those who had died, including animals. Dates noted when homes, buildings, and businesses had been searched for survivors, and other numbers counted the dead. There had been so many signs, posted on soaked, dilapidated rooftops or held in peoples' desperate hands, begging to be rescued. It was complete devastation.

All I could do as I watched the news broadcasts cry. It was the most sobering moment I'd ever experienced as an African American, in the only country I'd ever known. I was also very angry. I listened as native New Orleanians shared stories of their neighborhoods before the hurricane. They described vibrant communites, filled with lively people who loved and looked out for each other, where businesses kept the community going, and the culture was like no other. The image of President Bush flying in a helicopter over the top of these people as they cried out for help had been scored into my brain: an etching needle on a metal plate leaving an intricate, complicated design. It sickened me: the nation watching as Black people were left for dead in the Lower Ninth Ward of New Orleans.

Shockwaves rumbled all around campus. Many were furious about the country's response before and after the hurricane hit the city. Others argued that the logistics of getting rescue crews in was what caused the delay. Our campus welcomed students from Dillard and Xavier universities, whose schools had been flooded and destroyed. And so we heard firsthand what they had experienced, as they recounted their feelings of abandonment and horror. No food, no water, no shelter, no medication, and no way out. It was a pure tragedy. Our student body was outraged; it reminded us that we, as Black people, were still second-class citizens in America. I didn't know what I would do, but I knew I had to do something. I hoped that going on this trip would be a way for me to get inspired. Help me figure out how I would change the world.

"And thank you to those of you on this bus who are from Dillard and Xavier universities. We commend you the most, for you have been uprooted from your school, your community, and your families. As you work to settle in and continue your education, just know that we are here for you. We love you and we embrace you as our own. Franklin Forever!" Reggie shouted in closing, her fist high in the air.

And in our school's customary reply, with our fists in the air, the bus roared back, "Franklin Forever!"

BREATH HEAVY,

YET STEADY

first quarter

As THE HOURS passed, discussion ranged from gossip to radical activism and everything in between. I was amazed at how comfortable I felt talking with Melony. It rarely happened that way with women I felt an attraction to. I usually needed time to get to know them, then convince myself I wasn't attracted to them before I felt comfortable. For that reason, I tended to stay quiet and keep to myself; if it wasn't related to basketball, I rarely socialized with my peers. But her talkative, cheery personality made her easy to talk to. My eyes played ping-pong from her lips to her eyes down to her half-buttoned shirt, as easy as putting a ball in a hoop.

I listened to her as she spoke animatedly about how important it was for all people to try to help in some way—especially Black people. She was smart, passionate about her people, and beautiful. It was nice to sit and talk to someone like her. I felt the perspiration building in my armpits.

"I agree one hundred percent with Kanye West… our President does not care about Black people," she emphasized. "If he did, he wouldn't have been aloof and ignorant about the crisis that was visibly boiling over as the hurricane approached the Gulf Coast," she said.

"Yeah, there's no excuse for that," I had to agree. "We have enough resources to save the world, yet we couldn't save our own people?"

"That's because the people in the Lower Ninth aren't considered America's people. Fucking ethnic cleansing is what it is," she said.

We fell silent.

"I'm moving there once I graduate," she said, breaking the silence. "To New Orleans, I mean. I'm moving there and I'm going to teach and help rebuild the school systems there. That's my plan, anyway," she said.

What could I say? Her selflessness had me surprised.

"What are your plans?" she questioned.

My plans were a bit more far-fetched. I was too afraid of what others would think, so I worked diligently toward making them a reality, never sharing them aloud with anyone. I smiled shyly, looked away, then looked back at her. I cleared my throat.

"Well, I want to—I'm going to—I *plan* on playing in the WNBA. That's my plan." I looked down at my fidgeting hands.

"Nice!" she exclaimed with a smile. "Hopefully New Orleans will have a team by the time you're done. Then you can get drafted there," she added without hesitation.

I lifted my head and smiled bashfully. "Yeah, I hope so," I blushed.

We fell silent again.

Then, like the turn of the T.V. channel, she switched the conversation.

"Is it true that all the girls on the team are a bunch of lesbians?" she asked.

"No!" I defended with a nervous chuckle, and then rearranged my body in the bus seat, which suddenly felt cramped. "Ridiculous ass rumors—ridiculous even to believe, don't you think?" I questioned, putting the interrogation back onto her.

She waved it away with her hand.

"I know, I know, that *is* kind of ridiculous," she agreed, shaking her head and smiling. She seemed embarrassed but it didn't stop her. "Are you?" She asked it looking away, then looked back at me, then away again.

I glanced around the dark bus. Most of our classmates were asleep.

"What are you working on, a story for the school newspaper or something?" I whispered. "What's up with the third degree all of a sudden? What's up with these personal questions?" Irritated, I reached to pull my headphones over my ears.

She reached for my hand before I could cover them. "Hey. I didn't mean to offend you. Sometimes I can be too straightforward. I'm just curious that's all. I apologize. My bad. I'm being nosey," she said.

She continued to hold onto my hand. I looked down and finally snatched it away.

"It's cool. I'm cool." I swallowed hard and covered my ears with Jill Scott's soothing voice.

The last four hours of the trip were quiet between us. But I squirmed in my seat, feeling my heart thump excitedly between my legs.

———

At the Millions More March, spirits were high and the buzz was contagious. Louis Farrakhan and Erykah Badu spoke, amongst others, and preached and sang life and hope into the crowd. I was mesmerized by Badu's passion.

"We already have the power to change the world!" she called out to us. "Fear is the only thing holding us back!"

Her words, like her music, resonated and stirred me from within. I didn't quite understand how or why, but I felt stronger and more confident by the time she was finished. As she was preparing to leave the stage, she demanded that we put both fists in the air and scream out our own names. I did, without concern for who was watching me. I screamed as loud as I could.

One after another, each speaker commanded us to work diligently; to take control of our own communities by getting involved; and to band together as a united front. Emotions flared and the crowd erupted in frustration when the subject switched to the unarmed men and women of color constantly being gunned down and murdered by police across the country, without consequences. Farrakhan spoke about Hurricane Katrina and called for a class action lawsuit to be filed against homeland security's Federal Emergency Management Agency for its lack of action and neglect toward the people of New Orleans, too many of whom had lost everything, while thousands were dead. He called out the government's lack of effort to one: offer more assistance with evacuations before the storm hit; and two: support them with getting back the homes, schools, and businesses they lost.

The crowd was ignited. We knew we had a lot of work to do, and that it wasn't going to be easy, but the energy was electric and had everyone feeling like we could do anything. I stood on the National Mall and made a vow that if I made it to the WNBA, I would use my platform—my influence, my power, as Erykah Badu said—to begin the new world—one based in freedom, equality, love, and hope. It would be a place where those who were once oppressed rose up.

Melony and I didn't sit next to each other on the ten-hour bus ride back to Nashville. Things between us had clearly gotten awkward. We hadn't even hung out much over the trip. When a large group of us stopped at Ben's Chili Bowl, I mustered up the courage to stand next to her and ask her what she was going to order. She told me, but didn't ask me what I had in mind. I told her anyway. She didn't say much. I didn't force the conversation along. I just stood in the line and waited for my food. I ate with a broken off section of the group and she ate with the other. I watched her, though. She really was a talkative person, and it didn't seem to matter to whom she spoke—she talked to everyone and made friends quickly. I kept my interactions among the few classmates I already knew.

ZONED IN ON YOUR PRESENCE

CHEST HEAVING

UP AND DOWN,

UP AND DOWN

I CAN FEEL THE RHYTHM

OF THIS MOMENT

second quarter

WE MADE IT back to campus Sunday evening. Badu's words still echoed in my mind. I felt like I was still standing on that lawn watching her face magnified on the huge screens. I had been walking with my head held a little higher ever since. I can't explain how, but I felt more confident in myself.

Practice was early the next morning so I went straight to my apartment to unwind and rest up. Coach Reyes wasn't going to reserve any sympathies for my having been out of town, no matter what the cause or the reason. I had just gotten out of the shower and was about to eat the frozen pizza I'd put in the oven when I heard the knock on my front door.

I assumed it was one of my teammates wanting to know about the trip, but when I opened the door I saw Melony standing there. I froze. Everyone knew where the girls' and boys' basketball teams lived on campus; it wasn't hard to find me, but I was still shocked that she was standing at my door. Her big bright smile captured me again. Both of her hands were full: in her right hand she held movies, and in her left hand she held a bag of groceries.

She held up her right hand. "I have two classics: *Love Jones* and *A Bronx Tale*. Oh," she said, holding out her other hand, "and popcorn and beer. I just hope you're not busy," she finished with a wince, as if the wrong answer would physically hurt her.

I stood there in my robe—rigid, searching for words.

"Are you busy?" she asked again, a look of concern spreading across her face. "I figured, like me, you'd want to kick back and chill a little."

"No—no, I'm not busy," I finally said, scratching my damp hair. "I just cooked a pizza. I'm tired and I got practice early in the morning," I admitted. "I really wasn't expecting anybody."

"I know, I know, I know, I know, I know," she sang apologetically. "This was totally creepy, huh? I'm sorry. I'm sorry. I'm gonna go." She started to walk away.

"Well, uh—uh," I swallowed. "You're here now, you might as well stay. I don't mind having you here." I leaned my arm against the door, propping one leg over the other in some awkward attempt to look cool.

"*A Bronx Tale* is one of my favorite movies. I don't mind watching it again. Come on in."

She exhaled, and smiled. I slid to the side to let her in.

"I'll be right back. Give me one minute," I motioned with my index finger and went into my bedroom to change out of my bathrobe and slippers.

I came back out in one of my basketball t-shirts and baggy sweats. My apartment was a small one bedroom, one bath unit. The living room, a small square, was separated from the kitchen only by its counter. My dark green leather loveseat's back rested against it. In desperate need of furniture for my first apartment, my parents had bought it for me from a second-hand furniture store. The only other furniture in the matchbox living room was my thirty-two inch flat screen T.V., and a small round wooden coffee table. Posters of famous civil rights activists decorated my beige walls, alongside some of the best to ever do it in the WNBA—Lisa Leslie, Sheryl Swoopes, and Cynthia Cooper. A sliding glass door led to an intimately small balcony.

The only visitors I ever had were my teammates from time to time; limited friends allowed me to focus on basketball. Melony and I sat on the short leather loveseat like the departed red sea. We ate pizza, drank beer, and watched *A Bronx Tale*. I sipped my beer slowly. I didn't drink beer. I hated the taste of it. Plus, I'd seen what it did to some of my teammates after they'd been out partying. It never seemed worth it. I didn't want to be rude, so I drank it anyway. I watched her with quick glances. She wasn't shy about eating; she was on her fourth slice. I liked that she wasn't putting on airs like some girls did.

An hour into the movie an empty round baking sheet rested on the coffee table alongside two empty cans of beer. In an effort to get more comfortable, she slipped out of her shoes and folded her legs onto the couch, then tucked them underneath her butt. The waist of her jogging pants slid a little down her hips and revealed red and white polka dot boxers. Underneath those a lacey black thong showed.

I'd always wondered what kind of girl I would date if I could. But I never acted on those yearnings; I was too afraid of being alienated for being gay. I listened to conversations some of my teammates had with each other about what people said about them, the kinds of rumors that spread once people found out they were gay. Half the time they laughed it off because of how ridiculous they were, but I was mortified at the thought of people talking about me in that way. The girls on the team who were "out" were starters. They were popular and admired, their faces hung from banners on the stadium and around campus. People loved them! It seemed like their otherworldly athletic abilities and killer stats overshadowed almost anything they did off the court, or who they did it with. I was the third-string point guard, which was deficit enough. I didn't need any other drawbacks. I had to stay focused on my goals. This is the argument I drilled constantly into my mind.

I continued to watch Melony from the corner of my eye. Was she just awkward? Was she here trying to figure out the question she asked me days ago on the bus? Or was she just a groupie, trying to get into our team's inner circle any way she could? There were people who did whatever they had to in order to get with the stars everyone knew were headed to the WNBA— towards endorsement deals and million-dollar overseas contracts. But me?

With all these thoughts swarming around in my head my heart raced, and I struggled to ignore the igniting sensation that continued to grow between my legs.

"Hello? Where are you?" Finally I heard her question.

"My bad." I laughed. "I'm thinking about the long day I've got ahead of me tomorrow." I realized as soon as I released those words that I didn't want her to leave. I cringed regretfully. "What were you saying?" I tried to keep my cool.

"I was saying how crazy it is that people are always trying to tell other people *who* to love and *how* to love them. Like in this movie, where the Italian-American kid being in love with the Black girl is so wrong, like they're both not human or something, right? We should be able to be attracted to who we're attracted to, and love who we love, without judgment, right?" she finished, her eyes intently on me.

"Yeah." I shifted and squirmed a little on the tiny couch, then jumped up and went into the kitchen. "I don't really think about that stuff, though," I said as I moved away.

"Why not?" she turned towards me.

"My focus is on basketball. I have two years left to play. I highly doubt they'll be extending my scholarship for a fifth year. So that's my focus and priority. I'm trying to be like them." I pointed towards the posters of the women basketball players who lined my wall.

She chuckled. "Yeah, but you don't have Jordan up there!"

"Come on, now! That's a given. Of course Mike is the G.O.A.T! He's one of my all-time favorite players. But I'm not getting into the NBA," I joked as I surveyed my body. "This is sort of my shrine to the ladies of the game—the trailblazers. I wear twenty-three in honor of Jordan."

She smiled. "Okay."

I was glad to be off the topics of love and relationships.

"Speaking of trailblazers of the game, where's Cheryl Miller?"

I grabbed two more cans of beer from the refrigerator and tossed one to her. "Look at you! Whatchu know about the legendary Cheryl Dean Miller?" I teased.

"Well, let's see, at USC, Miller scored three-thousand-eighteen points, over fifteen hundred rebounds, seven hundred some odd free-throws made, and over four hundred steals. First *athlete* in USC's history to have their jersey retired. She also won a gold medal in the 1984 Olympics. She's a legend if there ever was one!"

"Well, damn!" I covered my mouth with my fist in astonishment. "You just go around with stats swarming in your head, huh?"

"Just the ones of those I admire," she blushed.

I chuckled nervously. "Well, I guess you *are* a fan of the game. Unfortunately, my little sister ruined my autographed Cheryl poster—haven't been able to get my hands on another one since," I said.

"Ooh, I know you were mad." She continued to survey the posters on my wall.

"*Pissed*. Still am," I assured her.

"Septima P. Clark, Nelson Mandela, King, X, Ella Baker, Assata Shakur, Angela Davis, and Huey P.— you got the all-star line-up right here!" She smiled with approval.

"Just a reminder of how I got here," I said honestly.

"Yeah. You know one thing that I guess isn't talked about often enough is the fact that these leaders were for *all* oppressed people. It's like Badu said this weekend, we have to stand up against oppression and hate."

"Yeah, I heard that, too. Her message definitely resonated with me. She was on point," I admitted.

"Including those oppressed for simply loving who they naturally wanted to love. So, if you down with them, you down with the upliftment of all oppressed people. You trying to be like them, remember? If so, you have to be more progressive in your thinking like she said." She stared at me hard, like she was checking I understood.

I flopped down next to her. I was feeling more relaxed after drinking the beer.

"I mean, I guess you're right. I haven't thought about it like that, really. But I can respect it. No one should be oppressed for any reason. Once I reach my goal, I'll have the power and influence she has and I'll do what needs to be done. But, like I said, I'm focused right now on one thing."

"How about you focus on the entire picture? We're all connected. You heard what Farrakhan said. We're all standing on the shoulders of our ancestors. These

women were able to break barriers in the game of basketball because of the greatness of women like Clark,
Baker, and Davis. They sacrificed everything. Believe
that," she said.

I gulped down some more of my beer, ignoring its
bitter, biting taste.

When the end credits rolled through and our eyes
struggled to remain open, we both agreed we couldn't
make it through another movie. I was relieved she
didn't want to since I would've definitely tried to stay
awake to remain in her company, but I couldn't help
but think about the grueling 5:00 AM practice I had
ahead of me, followed by classes. Besides, her sidebar
conversations were deeper than I was willing to go.

"How far are you from here? I can call you a campus escort. It's not a good idea for you to walk back
across campus this time of night by yourself."

"Oh, I didn't walk." She turned towards me. "I parked
right out front. That's really thoughtful, though," she
said in a tone I hadn't heard her use before.

"Should you be driving? You just drank three beers!"

"If you want me to stay, just ask, Taylor," she smiled
and blushed. I cleared my throat, stood up and stretched.

"Drinking and driving ain't cool for nobody." I said ignoring her comment.

She stood up and came closer to me.

"You're sweet. I like that." She looked at me hard again before gathering her things. "I'm good, though. I'm only going around the corner. If you give me your number, I can call you when I get in and let you know I made it…since you're all worried. And then the next time I decide to come over, I can call first. Okay?"

My heart pounded faster, and my hand shook slightly as I reached into my pocket and pulled out my phone.

I put her number in, then waited for her phone to buzz before walking her toward the door and opening it.

"Thanks for a great night," she said, turning back in the doorway. "I had fun."

"Yeah, same here for sure, I'm glad you came through." I smiled.

Before I could blink again, she had leaned her face into mine, and our lips were connected. Her mouth was warm. Unlike mine, her breath was slow and steady. I could taste the beer on her tongue. I forced myself to remain calm, fighting against the hot excitement that was surging within me.

She pulled away with a growing smile. "I thought so." She looked me slowly up and down, and then bit her bottom lip. "I hope we can do this again, Taylor."

She waved at me as she walked off down the hall.

I closed the door behind her, leaned against it, and exhaled. *Holy shit!*

I decided to take a cold shower to ease the flame growing in my loins. I turned on the cold water in the bathroom and heard a knock at the door. I headed back into the living room, scanning the counter and coffee table as she let herself in.

"I forgot something."

Melony closed and locked the door. She came in and gave me a single kiss on the lips.

"I—I—I don't know what I'm doing," I confessed.

"I know," she said calmly. "Let me show you." She placed her hand in mine and guided me into the bath-room where the shower ran.

I wish I could say I was incredible, but I nervously fumbled around like the anxious virgin I was. I had always imagined some magical moment where I would be as smooth as a Casanova lover, but I had no idea what I was doing. Our only saving grace was how cool she remained. Melony was patient as she showed me how to touch her, how to kiss her, how to hold her. She guided my perspiring, shaky hands with ease, allowing me to touch her in places I had only touched myself.

Finally; the moment I'd been longing for.

I AM ANTICIPATING YOUR NEXT MOVE

I KNOW WHAT YOU WILL DO

BUT WHAT WILL I DO?

CHAPTER FOUR
half-time

I PULLED MYSELF closer to Melony and we held each other under the covers in my bedroom. "I never imagined I would actually be able to do this with anyone," I confessed, smiling. "This feels so-so perfect. I'm trying not to get too comfortable with it—with you," I admitted. Melony frowned. "Why?"

"I don't mean it like that. I know it's only been a few weeks but you seem super chill and—and my heart still races whenever I see you. I'm walking around smiling for no reason," I chuckled. "I've dated before but it ain't never felt this good. I mean, whenever I hear my phone buzz my heart skips a beat at the thought that it could be you. Sometimes when I'm at practice, I'm not even there, I-I'm still here with you." The words came before I knew I'd said them. In the quiet after, as she took them in, I felt a stab of panic—what if I'd gone too far?

But she smiled and rubbed my face. "You just feel like you're in deeper than me because it's your first experience. Trust me, I feel the same. Sure, I don't have the first time jitters like you do, but trust me, I like you a lot, Tay. You're different," she said. "You're always on my mind, too. Why do you think I'm standing atch'your door waitin' for you right after practice, huh?" she laughed.

I smiled back but cleared my throat at the mention of it. "Yeah. About that…uh, maybe we—you shouldn't do that anymore?" She pulled back to examine my face. "It's just that you're there like, every day, and I bet people are whispering and wondering."

"So?" A flash of anger sparked in her eyes as she looked at me. "Let them! Most of your team is just like you, Tay. You do realize that, right?"

"Yeah, with their faces plastered all around the school. Don't nobody really care about them being like that. I'm just saying—"

"Tay," she interrupted, sitting up to look at me straight. "What are you afraid of? You don't trust me? I told you I'm staying low-key, too. You know my dad'll cut me off in a minute if he found out about you…about me."

"Yeah, and use his influence to have my ass kicked off the squad, too. I know how this works. I'm not trying to piss anybody off. Not your dad or my folks. I told you how my mom used to love, *love* Ellen Degeneres until—"

"Until she found out she was gay. I know, Tay. You've told me this story a bunch of times. Maybe your moms was just jumping on a bandwagon because she felt like that's how she was supposed to respond. You know Ellen's back now. People are changing."

I shook my head and sighed. "Not my mom. You had to hear how she was talking about her. Almost like she wasn't human. It's something I'll never forget."

"Well, that ain't you, Tay. You're not Ellen. You're your mother's daughter. She's going to love you anyway—and maybe she's secretly watching Ellen and don't nobody know it!"

We both laughed hard about that. Melony's soft lips kissed mine. "I'm worried, too. But I'm not about to let him run my life like that. I'm careful. I promise. You're safe," she smiled.

"Cool. Fine," I said reluctantly. "But can we agree to-to not meet in front of my room anymore? Please? Besides, I'm probably going to be staying later at the gym for a while anyway. I gotta learn these new plays and get more reps in. I *know* I'm better than Alicia. Yet she's coming off the bench and I'm still getting garbage time," I grunted.

"You *are* better than her. I don't know why the coach can't see that," she paused, looking at me thoughtfully.

"Exactly. I haven't been in the gym enough that's why. I need to show her I've improved, and that's the bottom line."

"Fine, Tay," she exhaled. "I know ball is life," she rolled her eyes. "I'm not trying to get in between you two," she smiled and nudged her shoulder against mine playfully, then conceded. "I love how dedicated you are to your game. Your passion is one of the things I love and admire about you. It's sexy," she licked her lips.

Her compliment pulled me into her and I melted into her arms. Melony had a way of making me feel defenseless.

"Just make sure you come to my room when you're done, then," she said in between kisses.

"I'll try. You know how tired I am after practice, Mel."

"Ooh, wait!" she jumped out of bed and rummaged through her backpack on the floor. She pulled out a piece of paper and handed it to me. "Here."

I took it. "What's this?"

"If you read it, you'll know! It's BSU: Black Student Union. I joined. You know, Reggie's got it together and we're actually *doing* stuff around the community this year. I mean, I really feel like going to D.C. changed something in me. I don't want to just sit around and complain anymore. We do food drives, help those suffering from homelessness, we tutor kids in after-school programs, we even have meetings with our school's president about issues on campus," she beamed.

I was secretly filled with admiration, and some other feeling I couldn't quite place at that moment. Melony hadn't just allowed the euphoria of the march to drain out of her. She was keeping it alive. She was doing something with it.

"So I guess that freshmen Reggie is alright then," I poked.

She rolled her eyes. "She's alright."

"That's cool." I handed the paper back to her.

"That's all you got to say?"

"What more do you want me to say? I think it's great, Mel. I love that you're still energized and doing your thing."

"You can, too, Tay. You can join." I didn't respond. "Well, if you joined, it—it could be another way for you and I to hang out together and we wouldn't have to worry," she said.

"Mel, when would I have time to do that? Seriously, coach already has the team signed up for volunteer days with specific organizations. Besides," I counted on my fingers as I ran through the list, "I got school, games, practice, tutoring, you—"

Melony's head jerked toward me.

"I didn't mean to say you're like a chore, don't go there," I pleaded. "You're the best thing about this year." I pulled her over to me with my sexiest grin, then wrapped myself around her on the bed. Her back was pressed against my body, my arms wrapped around her. I rested my head in the crook of her neck.

Her face drooped and her lips poked out like a child denied candy.

"Come on," I nudged her. "Let's keep doing this. I just don't have time for much else. Let's just make the best of the time we have together. Keep things simple like we said." I kissed her neck and turned her around toward me. "Cool?" I kissed her lips.

"You sure don't act inexperienced," she sighed.

"I had the best teacher," I winked. "Now, come teach me something else," I cooed, pulling her into the bed with me.

We kept our 'thing' on the low. We were both reluctant and unsure about calling it anything more. I loved that she understood my passion and focus was all about basketball, that everything else came a distant second. The thought of trying to be open and out for me was a huge cause of distress. The only rumors I needed getting back to the coaching staff about me were to do with my work ethic and dedication to my game. Melony had a lot to lose, too. Her father was the dean of the religion and philosophy department on campus. He, like the university, was conservative in thought and practice. They already had a strained relationship, mostly because she wasn't anything close to the conservative, reserved, traditional woman he wanted her to be.

We continued to go out on our strictly platonic-looking dates: public appearances that were always followed by the complete opposite. Whenever I wasn't at practice, or we weren't in class, we were together at my place. I loved everything about it, until one day, the conditions began to change. All of a sudden I *had* to meet her at my door by a designated time. I *had* to respond to her texts right after practice. She *had* to spend the night at my place and rarely at her own.

I became paranoid and started obsessing about whether people could see beyond the "friendship" we were carrying on. The thought of how my parents would react swung over my head like an invisible pendulum. Would this affect my chances on the team? Being gay was tolerated, not accepted. I was easily replaceable. So I forced changes in the way we did things: I had to get up too early to have Melony spend the night. I had papers to write, I had study groups to attend, or practice ran too late for me to do anything else other than crash. I snuck to her dorm late at night to avoid having her come to my apartment, and left too early to be seen.

Over the course of these months, the grueling drills, workouts, and practices continued, and the coaches began to notice my improvements—even made comments on it. I was eventually moved up to backup point guard. I was coming off of the bench—getting more playing time, being more efficient, making less mistakes. My hard work was paying off! I wasn't getting drafted but I had a chance of being accepted for workouts with some overseas teams if I kept things up—I might even get a shot at being invited to work out for some WNBA teams.

Basketball and school, basketball and school... there was only room in my life for these two priorities. At least that's what I told myself mattered the most. So I held Melony as far away as I could without completely pushing her out of my life.

GO TO MY RIGHT, GO TO MY RIGHT

I'M BETTER ABLE TO HANDLE YOU THERE

I GUIDE YOU THERE, TO MY RIGHT

CHAPTER FIVE
timeout

IT WAS EARLY morning. My hands and arms were clamped firm to the backs of her thighs while I devoutly licked her inner lips and stroked my tongue back and forth against her clit until her body began to pulsate. She released a loud satisfied cry and breathed deep, her chest rising and falling like a sprinter's at the ribbon. I scooted on top of her plump, naked body, and rested between her thighs where our vaginas met. She sucked my tongue hungrily at the sensation of me circling against her wet clitoris, faster and faster. My fingers slipped in and out of her between motions. Melony gripped my cheeks like basketballs and guided me faster and deeper into her. The sound of the wet rhythm exhilarated me. It felt electrical. We sang and shook simultaneously, until our stiff bodies collapsed on her bed. My entire body tingled.

Our heavy breathing starting to slow, I slid down her body and laid my head on her inner thigh and used her other thigh to cover my head completely. I buried myself there. I was safe.

"What do you want to eat?" I heard her muffled voice ask me. Our bodies still danced up and down from our breathing.

"Nothing," I responded quickly. "I have to go." I moved up and kissed her forehead, then jumped out of bed.

She groaned with displeasure. "Do you always have to leave like *right* right after? I can't ever hold you anymore?" She sat up and watched me slide into my jeans. "You must've worked up an appetite. We can go grab a quick bite, can't we?" she smiled.

Her question made me want to climb back into bed and between the safety of her legs again.

"Basketball is life," I bent over and kissed her on the lips and smiled.

"Tay, stop it. I'm serious. How can you just get up and leave after what we just did?"

"You don't want to hold me for too long. You might get too comfortable," I joked with a smirk. I sat on the edge of the bed to put on my socks and shoes. "Things are—they've been cool the way they are," I stammered.

"But I *want* to be comfortable with you," she mumbled.

I pretended not to hear her.

She sighed deep and finally blurted out, "I don't like things the way they are. Not anymore."

She sat up and held the cover tight to her breast, like I wasn't already familiar with her naked body. "I think I want more, Taylor. I'm not seeing anyone else and I don't want to. I love—" she stopped herself and seemed to choose her words carefully. "I love how you make me feel. I've never felt this way about anyone else. I look forward to you stopping by and us spending time together. I don't want to be fuck buddies anymore. I want more. I can't lie, I *want* to hold you and I want you to hold me! And I want you to *want* to hold me. We've been doing this for a while now, Tay." She looked into my eyes with seriousness.

Melony's words were hard for me to comprehend. I mean, I understood them, I just didn't know what to do with them. My feelings had intensified, too, yet I felt like I had them under control. I knew when and how to express what I was feeling for her. I thought we both did. I realized we could never have a relationship with each other; it was out of the question for me. I continued to lace up my shoes.

"Are you going to say anything?" she quizzed, in a tone of surprise and cautious demand. I stood up in my sports bra, my jeans open and my belt unbuckled. "I'm serious," she leaned out of the bed and tugged on my jeans. "I want you to stay," she begged.

I stood over her, looking into her eyes. My stomach flipped. I wanted to stay. I wanted to get back into bed and go inside of her until our bodies sang again. I wanted it all!

"Maybe next time. I really need to get to the gym," my words came out halfheartedly.

"Tay, it's five o'clock in the morning on a Sunday! I know there's no organized practice today, especially not this early. Come on!" she whined.

I sighed and contemplated whether I should reach for my shirt or pursue what seemed like the beginning of a serious battle. The playful, begging tone she had started with was gone; her face was firm and steady.

I sat on the edge of the bed and touched the side of her face. "Since when do you want me to stay like that?" I questioned in a playful puppy dog tone. I was trying to figure out her angle.

"Tay, I just want you to hold me—make me feel like you care. Remember that? Like we were at the beginning." She sat up further, still gripping the covers to her breast. "Even if it isn't true," she whispered.

"What," I exclaimed. "What do you mean, 'If it isn't true'? Where's all of this coming from? Melony, you know I care about you."

"How would I know that? It's almost been a year and you're still acting like you don't have any real feelings for me outside of sex. I have to beg you to stay and hold me. Are you really *that* afraid of what someone else might think of you? Who gives a fuck about them anymore?"

I couldn't believe my ears.

"Since when did you *stop* caring about what your father and his friends and his colleagues think around here? Don't try to pretend like I'm alone in this. Like there haven't been plenty of times when I wanted to kick it with you but you couldn't be seen with me because of your daddy and his *friends*." I threw up air quotes with my hands.

"You're right. But I'm getting tired of thinking about him over my own feelings, Tay. I'm not afraid of what I might feel if we just let ourselves be together completely without worrying. I want that. And I'm tired of pretending like I don't just because of what my dad thinks. This is my life!"

The knot in my throat made it difficult for me to swallow. Her words made me hard, wet—excited.

"I like things the way they are." I ignored the urge to jump out of my pants and back into bed with her.

"You do?" She sounded suspicious.

"Yes." I cleared my dry throat. My heartbeats quickened.

"So, this is all you want? Sex, nothing more? Your feelings haven't grown past that?" She appeared stunned.

"Look, Melony, if you don't like the way we're doing this then…I don't know." I sighed and shrugged. "This is all I can give you right now. I don't know why you would be expecting more anyway. We both agreed this is what it was going to be. I have feelings, too, but—"

"But what?" she pleaded, cutting me off.

"But—but—I mean, what are you asking for, a relationship? I'm not gay!" I blurted out.

She burst into a sarcastic laughter. "What?! You sure? That's funny because I thought having sex with me for—for *months!*—kind of put you into that category."

"W-well, you were wrong. I'm trying, Melony! I don't know what else to do," I admitted. Besides, my grades are starting to slip with all of these late nights and shit anyway," I lied again. "So—"

"I'm not asking you to tell the world tomorrow, Tay! Damn! Let's just admit it to each other first. Please." Her voice had got small again. "Think about how we met, Tay. Think about the voices from those podiums. They urged us to be strong, to be *real* to ourselves, to be the change we want to see. Think about all the women on your wall. We can be all of those

things we promised we would be just by being cou-
rageous enough to be ourselves right *now*, today. We
are the new world, Tay. Remember? Fuck everybody
else." she paused. "You keep talking about how Erykah
Badu is one of your all-time favorite artists, how she
touched your soul that day, and how you don't think
you'll ever be the same...but you ain't doing shit about
it," she shrugged.

"Melony, I—"The words were jammed in my throat.

I grabbed my t-shirt and pulled it over my head,
moving faster. I had to get out of her room—out of her
presence. I felt my throat ache from the boulder-sized
lump that had formed while I watched tears form in
Melony's eyes. I wanted to say more. I wanted to get
back into the bed with her and figure it all out. But I
didn't have the courage she wanted me to have...the
courage she had apparently found. And I wasn't going
to allow her to pressure me just because her feelings
had changed. She was the one reneging.

"I lo—I like you a lot, too, Mel. I really do. But,
Melony, you and I have an agreement. It's not like I'm
trying to play you. I can't be those people, I can't. I'm
not that strong. I'm just starting to figure things out.
Things are just *now* coming together for me. I'm glad
the march is still burning like a fire inside you and that
it's given you the strength you need. Just because I'm
not out there doing all the things you're doing doesn't
mean how I've felt since that day isn't real." I'm just

not—not ready." As I said it, I began to wonder what was the story to keep her from getting too close, and what was actually true.

She shook her head. "You're right. You're right." She cleared her throat, fighting through her cracking voice, fighting back her tears. "Let yourself out. I'm going to take a shower." She hopped out of bed and rushed into her bathroom, slamming the door behind her.

I snatched my jacket from her desk chair and ran out.

Walking away, I heard the voices in my heart tell me I was making a choice that wasn't my own. My mind traveled back to D.C., back to the National Mall, to the place where Erykah Badu had stood; I heard her soothing, peaceful voice:

> *Fear is false evidence appearing to be real. Change your thinking. Stop being scared! The new world begins in the mind.*

I exhaled, finding peace in those words momentarily. But the voice in my head told me I was doing the right thing. *Stay focused on your goals, Taylor. You're almost there. You'll have plenty of time to change the world.* My doubt was silenced. I sided with my head and kept going.

I CAN HANDLE YOU AND
ANTICIPATE YOUR NEXT MOVE

CHAPTER SIX
foul

MONTHS PASSED. I hadn't spoken to Melony since that early morning in her bedroom. I played the scene out over and over in my head almost every day, though. I couldn't get it out of my head. I thought about all the ways I could have responded—*should* have responded. I poured more and more of my time into basketball—spent so many days and nights in the gym working out to avoid being home—because being at home made me miss Melony.

I missed our conversations. I missed listening to her ideas about how the world should be. I missed how we laughed and joked around. I missed her smile, her touch, her voice, and her moans. And more than anything, I missed our friendship and the bond we built together. I wanted to call her and ask her to come over, but I knew what that would mean to her. It would mean more than I was capable of. I typed up text messages and erased them. I would stare at her name on my cell's screen with my thumb over the call button, but the fear of what she wanted from me kept me from pushing it. Instead I practiced drill after drill, and studied our playbook like I was preparing for a final exam. I ran plays in an empty gym with my invisible teammates.

When our team's starting point guard injured her ankle in the first half of a game, I was no longer an every-now-and-then third option. I was coming off the bench regularly and playing extended minutes. After the game I called home to share the news with my parents. Then, unconsciously, I dialed Melony's number. It felt natural for me to want to share the news with her. I longed to hear her voice repeat my stats back to me, critique areas of the game where I could've played better. I'd played fifteen minutes, scored ten points, had six assists and one rebound. I knew she would be happy for me.

It rang twice before I realized what I had done. I panicked and pressed the "end" button before she answered, went home and ate an unfulfilling frozen dinner. I kept my phone nearby, staring at it and hoping she would call...hoping that she had seen the game and wanted to congratulate me, or that she saw my missed call and wanted to return it. But she didn't.

———

It was a crisp and clear late afternoon on campus. The sun was almost gone from the sky. Its fading presence pulled in the tall buildings' shadows. Leaves were falling, some blowing across the gray concrete in a hurry. Their bright orange, yellow, red, and green litter brought a hot-cider-apple-pie-fleece-throw feeling to campus. Jackets, sweatshirts, hats and skullcaps adorned my classmates' bodies. Some walked like it was rush hour; others sat in the grass like it was summer. There were those who walked like they had no place to go, and a trio played ball on the well-watered grass. I was leaving another grueling practice. All I wanted to do was hit the shower and then my bed. I thought about the term paper I had to write before next week, the math test I had coming up, and our next game against a top seeded team. Would I be able to start this game? Hell, would I even get any real minutes?

I walked with Jay-Z blasting through my headphones, the hood of my oversized hoodie pulled over my head. Before I knew it, I'd bumped into two women who seemed attached at their hips. Embarrassed, I began to apologize profusely, and helped one of them pick up the books I caused her to drop. The evening's air was crisp and cool, but when her face settled into my view, I felt like hot lava ran through my insides.

I whipped the hood from my head. "Melony?" My eyes darted between the both of them. "*Williams?*"

"Hey, Dawson," Williams greeted me with a smile and a nod. "Don't sweat it." She put her arm back around Melony.

I shoved the last book into Melony's hands. She avoided my eyes. "What are you up to Melony?" I grilled through clenched teeth, trying to stay calm. "I haven't seen you around in a while."

"Been busy," she replied sharply, looking up at Williams with a smile.

"Dawson, go home and get some rest. Friday may be another big game for you," Williams grinned as she patted me proudly on the shoulder.

"We don't know if McLemore'll be ready, so you gotta be," she instructed, oblivious of my focus on Melony.

"Yeah," I said dryly, my eyes still focused sternly on Melony.

They moved past me, Williams' arm comfortably around Melony's shoulder, pulling her in tight. I stood and watched them until they were out of sight.

I couldn't get home fast enough. My hands trembled. I could barely get the key into the lock. Inside of my apartment, I threw my book bag across the small living room floor, where it slid and slammed into the wall with a bang. I put a frozen dinner in the microwave but I'd lost my appetite. I sat on my loveseat and watched the meal grow cold on the round coffee table. Finally, I decided a shower would help calm my nerves.

Still, my mind raced there. What was Melony doing with Raquel Williams, my teammate—the starting power forward on my team? I paced back and forth in my bedroom. Everyone knew Raquel Williams; "R-Dub". She was known for her triple doubles. Williams was all but guaranteed a first round draft pick into the WNBA. She dominated at her position—in our division and across the nation. She was open and unapologetic about dating women—and she dated a bunch: tall girls, short girls…blondes and brunettes, thick girls and skinny girls. She didn't seem to discriminate. I'd see her walking with her arm draped around so many shoulders like I'd seen her do with Melony. Each time the girl looked like she believed she was the only girl in Williams's world—the same way Melony had looked.

Was she serious? Was she just going to go from sleeping with me to the next available basketball player on my team? The more I tried to make sense of things, the more upset I became. I lay down on my bed because regardless of my emotions, my body was sore and tired. I needed to rest. But there I was, restless. I couldn't slow my mind. I had to talk to her. I had to know what she thought she was doing with *my* teammate. Upset and desperate for answers, I reached for my cell phone and called her. The phone rang so many times I thought I'd get her voicemail. Finally she picked up.

"Hello?"

"Don't pretend like you don't know who this is. What are you doing, Melony?"

"Tay?" she asked, sounding unsure.

"Don't act like you don't know it's me! You saw it was me before you answered!"

"As a matter of fact I didn't. I erased your number a long time ago. Now, what do you want?" she asked with a sharpness void of patience.

"A long time ago? It hasn't been that long, Melony."

She exhaled impatiently. "Why are you calling me? What do you want?"

"What do you mean, *what do I want*? You know why I'm calling. What the hell are you doing with Williams? What, are you...you dating *her* now?"

"*Now*? Don't try to pretend like you and I was ever dating—or like we were anything for that matter—so don't worry about who I'm dating, or who I'm hanging around with. Do me a favor and lose my number."

"Really, Melony? Since when?" I yelled.

"Since when what?" she yelled back. "Since when what?!"

"Since when did you start treating me like you don't know me? You know why I'm upset. You're bogus! You go from fucking me to fucking my teammate? How messed up is that?"

"Tay, you and I had an arrangement, remember? That arrangement is over. What? You thought I was going to sit around and wait on your ass?" She laughed out loud before I heard her line click.

"Melony!" I yelled into my phone but it was too late; she'd already hung up.

I jumped up and paced back and forth in my bedroom, letting out growls of anger and frustration. I wasn't done. I was so angry I called her back. She didn't answer. I called her again. No response.

So I texted her.

Taylor

> I knew you were nothing more than a groupie. Something told me that the moment you sat next to me on the bus. Groupies don't become wives. Just remember that.

Melony

> If I were a groupie I wouldn't have sat next to your third string ass.

Taylor

Groupies don't become wives.

Melony

Jealous much? It doesn't look good on you. Shouldn't you be at the gym "working out"? Lol!!

Taylor

This whole thing's a joke to you, huh? Well, she can have my sloppy seconds.

Melony

What? Oh, so just because I decided to be with someone who has time for me, I'm a groupie and a hoe? Get real! Go find yourself.

Taylor

Oh, you've found yourself? Or do you think you've found your ticket? Either way, I wonder what your daddy's gonna say about this...

Melony

Lol...you're real sad right now. He said he'll continue to pray for me, just like I will for you! Try again. I wanted to wait for you. I was willing to take it slow, but you didn't even want to do THAT. Now you're acting like we had something. An AGREEMENT was all it was, remember? So please stop with this weak ass charade. I haven't seen or spoken to you in months! I'm going to sleep. Please leave me alone!!!!

Taylor

You're right. But out of all the girls on campus, you chose to mess around with MY TEAMMATE? What part of that is OK?

Half an hour passed without a reply from her.

Taylor

Hello? Are you awake?

Five minutes later I pushed harder:

Taylor

I'm coming over.

I PRESS MYSELF FIRMLY INTO YOU

THERE'S MORE HERE THAN SHOULD BE

THIGH FEELING THE

MUSCLE OF YOUR BACKSIDE

YOU SWITCH AND FACE ME

third quarter

OF COURSE I didn't go over to her house. I was only pushing for a response. I wanted to go over there and talk to
her, but yet again I found myself paralyzed by fear. What
was I going to say? Besides, she was with R-Dub now,
and I was clearly a distant memory.

That thought left a hole in my heart and head.
I tried to stay focused in my classes; nevertheless I
couldn't stop myself from languishing over what it
would have been like had I given Melony and I a real
chance. Would it have been so bad if I had just thought
about what I really wanted, as opposed to what people
wanted for me? Why could I not just stop thinking
so much about what people thought about my own
life? How could I call the great leaders on my walls
my heroes if I didn't even live honestly as who I was?
What was the point of going to marches, yelling and
screaming and crying at the injustice, if I wasn't going to come back and fight for myself? Badu had said
that people always thought that what they were going
through was heavier than what anyone else was facing. I knew she was right; I had to look at myself in
the mirror, because that was where the change had to

begin—with me. It started with me loving myself as much as I loved ball.

I thought again of Williams. She was a star. She didn't worry about that stuff—but, I argued with myself, she didn't have to worry about that. Everyone loved her regardless. She'd taken the team to the final four last year. She was on the ESPN highlights. She was going into the WNBA, virtually guaranteed. I had barely made it as a backup. I still played limited minutes and accumulated few stats worth recalling.

All I wanted was for my hard work to pay off. I'd convinced myself it was the only thing I truly needed.

But when I saw Melony smiling and cozied up with Williams, it became plain to me, without a doubt, that I also wanted Melony.

I was a young woman living on my own. It was time for me to let go of my fears and have a relationship with someone I actually wanted to be with. My mom would always ask me if there was some special guy I was seeing—then warn me not to put so much into basketball that I ended up "marrying Wilson."

"You know dribbling Wilson won't get me grandbabies, Taylor," she would always say through her laughter.

I imagined how my mom would react if I told her that I had feelings for a special lady. Would it be so bad...if I told my mom the truth? Would she banish me from her life like she had Ellen? Only speak of me in negative, disappointed terms? It didn't matter if Williams was a star, if I wasn't a star, it didn't matter. My fear was wrapped up in what other people thought—in comparing myself to people who didn't matter. I just had to stop fucking caring. I realized then that the words I had heard at the Millions More March were seeds that had been planted in my soul; finally, they were beginning to grow. It was time for me to put my old thinking behind me. I needed to become my own leader—a new world for me in and of itself. It wouldn't be easy, but I was determined.

I rushed out of class and practically jogged back to my apartment, hoping not to bump into Melony or Williams again. But apparently, it was inevitable. As I turned the corner leaving the math building, I walked directly into Melony. She looked happy and beautiful. Melony knew just how to accentuate her beauty. Her lips, made up with red lipstick, looked fuller. Her curly hair was wrapped up in a colorful headscarf that made her look like a queen. She wore heels and blue jeans with a short leather jacket, open to reveal a collared shirt unbuttoned low and showing her full, round breasts.

I couldn't help but stare. Memories played on the projector screen of my mind.

"I thought you said you were coming over."

"I was…I-I changed m-my mind, I guess," I stuttered.

She pushed past me, using her shoulder to bump me. "Right."

I whipped around, grabbed her wrist, and pulled her in close to me. "Where are you going?" I asked low, hoping to avoid a scene. I held on tight to her wrist.

She was startled. "Ow, Tay, you're hurting me," she cringed, her eyes flashing wide at me.

"Leave Williams alone," I threatened.

She smirked. "So now you care? Now you want to hold me? Girl, let go of my damn arm!" She tried to pull away, but I gripped her wrist even tighter.

"Don't try to make a scene," I warned.

"You're the one making a scene," she frowned, speaking in a more aggressive tone. "Now let me go!" she demanded.

"Listen, and I'll let you go. Leave Williams alone or I'll—"

"You'll what?" she said low, cutting me off, puffing her chest up into my face and sending her scent to my nose and my mind to happier times. The moment excited me; all I really wanted to do was hug her, kiss her, and tell her how sorry I was. I stared down into her shirt and never saw it coming.

Williams came running across the quad and pushed me so hard my body slammed into the concrete of the building behind me.

"What the fuck is going on over here, Dawson? Is there a problem?" Williams' face stared down at me. She folded her arms and stood protectively in front of Melony, waiting for my explanation.

I was five feet ten; she stood towering over me at six feet five, but at that moment it didn't matter to me. Neither her height nor her strength—not even the fact that she was my teammate mattered to me in that instant. I saw flashes of black; flashes of red. I felt the heat rising inside my chest.

"Yeah, there's a problem! This is *my* girl you fucking!"

I pushed Williams back, and she stumbled into Melony. Then I swung at her and connected.

The fight seemed to last forever. I lost my sense of time and place until I looked up to find campus police separating us, and pulling my arms behind my back.

I couldn't recall the punches, scrapes, and scratches, but I felt them as I sat in Coach Reyes's office with Williams next to me. I was in pain. I gave Williams a once over. She sat, breathing hard, still steaming, but she didn't have so much as a mark on her. Except for some of her cornrows being unraveled, she didn't look like she'd been in any type of physical altercation—more like a hard morning's workout. It was obvious who had won the fight. I slumped even lower into my seat. I was embarrassed and disappointed. Most of all my head throbbed right alongside my anxious heart. Would I be benched, or worse, kicked off the team?

Coach Reyes was a former college basketball star who became a coach right after graduation. She was known as the third winningest coach in our division—we'd only lost one game this year. She was no-nonsense, no matter who you were: if you didn't work hard, you didn't play, period. She came from a hardworking Mexican-American and African-American family. She was in her office by 6:00 AM every day, right after working out at the gym. Her system was simple: be consistent, put in the work, create your foundation from the fundamentals, and the efforts will pay off in every part of your life, not just on the court.

She sat looking at us now from across her desk: all six feet, eight inches of her (with heels on, which she wore every day). Her long, shiny black hair was pulled back as always into a ponytail. She was beautiful, and always perfectly manicured. When I first arrived I fell hard for her beauty; but after two weeks of suicide drills her beautiful looks took a backseat to my respectful desire to show her I was there to work hard and win.

You didn't want to do anything to embarrass her, the team, or the school. And you certainly didn't want to be on her bad side. But here I was. Definitely on her bad side.

Coach Reyes turned toward the open window behind her. Whenever she was in her office, she wore a tailored suit. Today was no different. Her suit jacket sat draped over the back of her brown leather chair, and her long sleeved, silk shirt was rolled mid-way up her muscular arms. She turned back around, scooted up to the desk, clasped her hands together, and cleared her throat. Her eyebrows almost seemed to touch; her eyes, squinting in disapproval, focused in on us like laser beams. They appeared capable of reading our souls. She continued this death stare between Williams and I for far too long. My breaths shortened and my heartbeat felt faint. I felt like I was beginning to suffocate under the silence. We both released a heavy sigh when she finally spoke.

"First, I'd just like to say you both are suspended from our next game. And you both owe me five thousand suicides for saving your asses from being expelled and even jailed. Fighting on school grounds," she paused and sighed, "is against the law, first and foremost, and against player policies. But you already know that. I guess handling that—that *shit*, whatever it was, behind closed doors, like young adults, wasn't an option?" She paused to throw looks of disappointment our way once more. "I mean, how *could* it be an option? What you two were settling was—was life altering, right?" she asked rhetorically. "Well, as you both know—and seem to care so much about—the next game is one of our biggest yet—and neither of you will be there to help us win." She sighed and shook her head. "You've jeopardized your basketball careers here at this university, not to mention the reputation of your team and school.

"Is this the face of the lady Panthers? Let me be clear. No, it is not. We are a family here, and as a family we settle and handle our shit in house. In house!" She raised her voice as her index finger hit the desk with each word.

"Do you understand?" she questioned with sternness.

We opened our mouths to speak—

"Of course you do!" she yelled, slamming her right hand onto the desk, then quickly returning both hands to the clasped position with renewed calm. "I don't know, and I *really* don't care, why the two of you were fighting, but one thing I do know and can rest assured of, is that you have resolved it. I know it's been resolved. Suspensions can always be indefinite, right? Right. Williams!"

Williams jumped and sat up taller, her hands in her lap, mimicking Coach's perfect posture. Coach Reyes's attention rested on Williams and she took another contemplative pause.

"As one of the captains of this team I cannot begin to express my disappointment in how you handled yourself today. No matter what, you should've kept your composure. You've been with us for four years. Four years. I know we've shown you better than this. And Dawson," she didn't even look to me, "for all the work you've put in to get to this point with the team, only to create an unnecessary, major setback like this is...is unbelievable."

She shook her head in disbelief. "I mean it's really beyond me. If I can't trust you off the court, I certainly won't take my chances with you on the court—not leading *my* team. I was just getting to the point where I felt like I *could* trust you. You have a stellar work ethic, and it shows, so I know you have a higher level of discipline than this." She paused. "I have nothing further to say. What I need is for the both of you to get the hell out of my office. I'm expecting your five thousand suicides recorded and on my desk by Friday. Be prepared to address your teammates tomorrow. They will want to know why you have failed to put us and winning the championship first. They deserve an explanation. You're dismissed." She turned her chair toward the window.

We mumbled our deepest and sincerest *Thank-you*s and *Sorry*s and disappeared from her office like ghosts.

I hurried in the opposite direction from Williams, feeling like shit.

Not only did I regret what had transpired; I was deeply embarrassed after the ass whooping Williams gave me. In the coach's office I realized I had allowed my emotions to actualize my deepest fear. My stomach was in knots. I was anxious; afraid about what would happen next. I wanted to head home, clean myself up, and sleep it off. I threw my hoodie over my head and walked fast. I felt someone's hand rest on my shoulder.

"Hold up."

I turned around quickly. My heart began to race.

"You heard coach say we have to clear this shit up, so that's what we're going to do, you feel me?" Williams looked down directly into my eyes.

I sighed, realizing the fighting was over, and thanking God she wasn't ready for round two. But I didn't respond. I honestly didn't know what to say.

"Well, look, I'm not in the business of fighting over these broads. They're a dime a dozen. I'm sorry for all that. You should've spoken up. I didn't know she was your girl. I didn't know you were—you know." She paused. "Well, I *did*," she quickly added, "just not with *her*."

"I-I'm not—she's not—"

Williams stepped back with her eyebrows raised and arms crossed. "Right, right, right. Well look, I got your back. I've known for a while now, a bunch of us did. We just didn't want to be all up in your business and shit. We know how it is. You don't have to worry about us running out of here and talking shit about you behind your back. You gotta learn to open up and trust somebody. If you gon' trust anybody it should be us. You wouldn't of gotten your ass kicked today had you spoken up, you feel me?" she chuckled.

I frowned. I didn't like the fact that she was throwing it in my face.

She shook her head at my silence. "How long have you been my teammate? Three years? And you see me, you know who I am, I'm not hiding. That shit eats you up on the inside. We a family. I know you're all quiet and reserved and shit, but I thought you knew that. I mean, yeah, sometimes we argue and maybe even fight, but at the end of the day we are still a *family*. That means you can trust us. You hearing me?"

I nodded like a kid sister still trying to find my words. "I'm sorry for overreacting. I just—"

"Don't sweat it, Dawson. My girl—my *real* woman—she goes to a different school. I'm just having a little fun. I don't need this going any further than the coach's office and this locker room, right? So now you know a secret about me. We're even."

She reached her hand out and I took it. We slapped hands before she pulled me in for an embrace.

"Meet me tonight, say around ten, and let's get some of these suicides out of the way. Unless you want to go back to the end of the bench, you feel me?" She turned to walk away with a chuckle.

"Williams," I called to her.

She turned around. "What's up, Dawson?"

I responded with silence, my mouth unable to produce the words.

"I told you, don't sweat it." She waved me off. "We've all been there in one way or another. Just remember, we're family. You'll see. See you tonight. Don't be late."

KNEES BENT, TORSO LOW

ARM OUT WAVING–

ATTEMPTING DISTRACTION

NO REACHING,

I'M NOT READY TO TAKE IT

MY HAND FIRM ON YOUR SIDE

FIRMER ON YOUR SIDE,

I GOT

YOU

fourth quarter

"**WE'LL KEEP IT** short and sweet tomorrow, D. We'll tell them we got into a confrontation about basketball and let it get the best of us. That way you don't have to tell all your business and shit, feel me?" Williams counseled as we left the gym.

We were headed into the locker room. Without hesitation, I gratefully agreed with the plan.

When I walked into the locker room, my teammates were changing for practice. My head felt like a wet sandbag. I couldn't seem to lift it up. I avoided eye contact with everyone. I walked quietly toward my locker. One of my teammates started clapping loudly. I looked up and saw it was our starting center Dalany Gibson. Then another teammate joined in, our backup small forward, Lisa Thomas. Then Kelly Rice, our shooting guard, joined in. I looked around as the rest of the ladies joined in. Soon the locker room was loud with applause and hooting. I stood in front of my locker and put my gym bag down. The ladies circled around me, clapping louder and bursting into laughter as they tapped me on my butt, my back, and rubbed my head in a sort of congratulatory moment.

My face flushed warm, I smiled nervously. "What's

going on?" I asked, slightly flustered.

"We're proud of you, Dawson—for finally coming out of the damn closet!" Dalany Gibson hooted, then gave a high-five to Lisa Thomas.

"Yeah, Dawson, we thought you were gonna die of suffocation in that mug!" Lisa joked. There was more loud laughter.

Gibson approached me and placed her hand on my shoulder. "Don't worry, though. You're safe. You don't have to hide in here. You're among people who love and care about you. You *should* know that. Now, we're not all dating women in here," Gibson stood back and smiled wide, "cause I'm strictly dickly," she said squatting low and popping her butt out in a gyrating motion. A few others danced over and started slapping her butt with their towels, jumping and dancing and laughing heartily.

"Okay!" I heard a few of them proclaim proudly.

"All right, chill out and go get those damned suicides done! Coach said if y'all don't get it done by Friday, the rest of us will have to help you," Rice called over with her back to me. She was putting on her practice gear. "And if that happens," she turned towards me, "then I'll have dibs on that ass." She hooted and slapped hands with Williams who was seated at her locker changing, staying very quiet.

I felt a sense of calm come over me. I had tossed and turned all night long trying to figure out what I would say and how I would say it. I was so relieved when Williams gave me the words to say. She didn't care that we fought. She cared more about protecting me, and my personal space. Damn, that really touched me.

I had spent so much time building an impenetrable wall of safety and security around myself, I never felt like I could let anyone in to the real me. Yet, as I stood there, I didn't feel ostracized. I didn't feel judged or rejected. And suddenly, I wasn't really sure why I'd done it this way in the first place. My teammates supported me in practice, and on the court, so why wouldn't they support me off the court, too? Somehow I could never see it. I couldn't look over the wall of my own insecurities and fears of rejection. For the first time I looked around—I mean, I really looked around—at my teammates. I just stood and took it all in. For the first time I realized I wasn't just a part of a team. We were a sisterhood. I was a part of a sisterhood, and I was finally willing and ready to embrace them.

I smiled at Williams. She shook her head and gave me an *I told you so* smile in return.

"Don't worry, Rice, I'll get mine done. It's *her* you have to worry about," I said slinging my jersey toward Williams. "Dub was running super slow this morning. Besides, one beatdown's enough for me." The locker room erupted with laughter and jokes. For the first time I allowed myself to relax in the laughter and love that, honestly, happened all the time in that room, whether we won or lost. I was the one who'd pushed that love away from me—away from the real me. I had become skilled at basketball, and skilled at keeping people on the other side of my wall. I had failed to consider the amount of love and support I was pushing away. I looked around and breathed a sigh of relief. I allowed the escaping breath to carry with it the weight of my old world.

As I was changing into my practice gear my cell phone buzzed. I reached into my gym bag and pulled it out, then stared down at Melony's name, and her message below it.

Melony

Are you OK, Tay?

My cheeks flushed warm and the stinging water threatened to escape my eyes.

Thinking of Melony took me right back to the Millions More March. We each went for different reasons, and we found each other. I had made promises on that trip that when I became someone people admired I would be able to help others. As if I needed to be someone else in order to be myself—to be better. I thought about how empowered and inspired I had felt there, but I hadn't understood then how much people have to sacrifice in order to change things, big or small. They gave up their careers, their families, and even their lives to fight for what's right. How could I help change anything if I couldn't start by being brave enough to be myself? *No more hiding, Taylor*, I thought to myself. I threw both of my fists in the air and screamed my own damn name. "Taylor Marie Dawson!" And with my teammates staring, I ushered in my new world.

I smiled and placed my phone back into my bag.

———

Later that evening, I wobbled from my couch to answer my door, ice packs taped tightly to my knees. After practice, Williams and I had decided to complete some of our assigned drills. My knees were screaming from the pounding intensity of it all.

Lisa told me she'd come down and watch ESPN's *His and Hers* with me. I was looking forward to her company.

"Hey," Melony smiled at me.

"Hey," was all I could say in response.

"Did you get my text?" she asked.

"Yeah, I got it." I pulled my phone out of my pocket and stared at it, like the message had just come in.

"Well?" she quizzed.

I swallowed hard. "Yeah, I'm—I'm good."

Her arms were behind her back; she stretched them out to me, revealing her offerings.

"I have something I think you might like," she smiled. "*The Cider House Rules*. And of course, popcorn...but no beer," she giggled nervously. "Do you mind if I come in?" Her eyebrows were raised and her eyes were wide with anticipation.

My shoulders instinctively relaxed. I melted on the inside. No more wall.

I still heard the voices in my head. I still felt the pull of her question on my heart. I listened to both voices...only this time, I decided to listen to my heart.

"Come on in," I smiled wide and stepped aside.

She walked in and I closed the door behind her.

MY EYES LOCKED IN ON YOURS

YOUR EYES FLASHING BACK

LIKE LIGHTNING

I FORGET MY POSITION

LET MY GUARD DOWN AND LET YOU

PASS ME

I'M HELPLESS

AND SURRENDER

I GIVE IN

TO THE INEVITABLE

THESE POINTS WILL BE YOURS...

MY TURN NOW

SURRENDER

A PROSE POEM BY VERDE ARZU

"I can hear your heart beating." Those were the words you spoke to me last night as you sat cradled in my arms, your left ear pressed firmly against my chest. I played with those words as they left your lips and entered my mind; I turned them around and thought of how one feels when given the opportunity to hear another human being's heart beat. The wonder that comes when one realizes that they are listening to life.

In my twenty-five years I have come to find that we have to learn to listen to the beat of our own life and follow it, no matter how challenging it becomes. I have been listening to the rhythm of life and it's the most beautiful and complicated rhythm I have ever heard. I have learned that when life seems to be going too fast or too slow, or too much is happening, or not happening enough, we are simply offbeat. When you're offbeat you know it and perhaps everyone else does, too. You are an essential part of why I'm enjoying the harmonious, tantalizing beat of my life.

Last night was great. We sat facing each other with our legs crossed on my bed in the dark. The smooth, relaxing, neo-soul sounds of the African-French sisters played softly in the background. I sat and watched as you rolled; I didn't care about your technique because I enjoyed the way your tongue ran across the dark brown cigar wrapper.

Your lips glistened, highlighted from the streetlight that came through my blinds. I wondered to myself as you concentrated on applying the finishing touches if my lips would ever be able to touch yours again. You looked up, smiling, catching me staring with such intensity that my thoughts could only have been sexual. You grabbed your lighter, and as the flame lit the paper, you leaned forward, staring directly into my eyes, and slowly placed the blunt into the small crack between my parted lips.

As I smoked, my mind raced through incomplete thoughts until it slowed on the night before:

We were holding each other in my bed, half asleep, when I felt your full lips press against mine. The moment ended all too quickly—I didn't have a chance to respond. Maybe I was dreaming, I thought. My eyes grew heavier and I felt myself drifting back into the first realm of unconsciousness, but I woke again because you bit down softly on my bottom lip. I jerked away, not knowing if I'd be able to control myself— knowing, in fact, that I would not.

What am I doing anyway? I asked myself. But it felt so good that the question left as quickly as it came. My body tensed; I was aroused, yet my mind was crowded with thoughts. Never had I laid with someone and it felt so right. I inhaled, exhaled, allowed my body to relax.

As my thoughts settled I realized we were staring into each other's eyes again. I noticed the corners of your lips as they turned up slyly, as if you had just outwitted me in a game. I continued to stare. I wondered about the thoughts that lay behind your dark brown eyes. I wished I could hear them. Your eyes were mysterious, revealing, and sensuous. Your long curled lashes danced around your bedroom eyes. I wanted to be able to look into them and hear your soul—hear your soul speak of the secrets nestled beyond the softness of your mother earth.

At that very moment fear encapsulated my entire being. I liked you too much, too soon, too everything.

What am I doing? I thought again.

First of all, I barely knew you; we hadn't been into it—whatever *it* was—longer than a month. Like every other person who entered my life and shared an intimate moment with me, I wondered what your intentions were. Where was this going? I wanted to get up and run. Run from finding out. Because maybe I'd be disappointed at the discovery. What if I found out I was just interesting enough for you to pass some time with? We had already agreed that neither of us wanted anything beyond friendship. Yet here we were.

My mind raced again with the weed and the questions. The questions I posed to myself made me want to lie down. I found myself stretched across my bed, wondering how to keep my feelings, which had ventured so far beyond friendship, tucked away. I was undeniably attracted to you. But there was more. The more I got to know you, the more I was drawn to you. Drawn to the way you pulled your shoulder-length, burgundy-tipped locks back into a ponytail. Drawn to your brown skin, your evenly arched eyebrows, your dimples and the way they accented your commercial-perfect smile. Drawn to the melanin in your skin—a gift—added beauty from your travels under the West African sun. To your short slender fingers, and your manicured nails that shone. To the way you stood four inches shy of me at a mere five-foot-one. To your arms, toned from your early morning routine of weightlifting and running.

I recalled when you texted me and asked me to join you on your run. You stuck to your usual speed as I lagged willingly behind. I watched the Spandex, clinging to each stride, outline even the deepest curves of your waistline, your toned hips and runner's thighs. You turned around without missing a beat, all skill and practiced technique. My eyes slowed as I watched your breasts contained only by your sports bra. They moved to a musical number all their own—your body became a new symbol in the collection of notes that signified a beat on my scale. With each motion I heard a new and invited sound. I found myself caught up in you—I didn't want to be caught up in you, but I did.

It was easy. Within a few short weeks I found myself being touched, held and kissed by you. Damn, you're good. Or was I just long past ready?

Was it that I enjoyed your company too quickly? Was there something wrong with that? I honestly didn't know. Were you running game on me? Were you intentionally drawing me in to have sex with me? Sex would definitely be a bad idea...I didn't want to wrestle with the deep emotions I knew were going to come after a night of passion with a woman for the first time. I wasn't ready, so I had to control myself.

My thoughts were interrupted by the soft sound of your voice asking me if I was okay. Rhetorical it seemed, as you didn't wait for a response. With the language of confidence you placed your hand on my thigh and moved it up my behind and across the small of my back. I closed my eyes, escaped in silence to enjoy the moment. Only a moment, though—I was afraid of losing control.

Was I thinking too much? Was I wrong to want to trust you, or right not to? Had I, in finally finding someone I was truly attracted to and interested in, forgotten how to act? Had I ever known? Goosebumps covered my body. I felt your fingertips pass through the tight curled roots of my hair to my scalp, and you massaged my head. My mind continued to flood with incomplete thoughts.

Control yourself, was all that was left.

It was all I had left; all I had to keep myself from turning over and surrendering to you.

Thank you:

First, thank God! Additionally, thank you to my ancestors who guide me. Specifically, Granny y mi padre, Adolfo Arzu. Thank you to my mom whose gift of writing manifests itself through me. Mom, your love and support are endless.

Thank you to the greatest brothers a sister could ask for: James Green and Sterling Green! Thank you for your belief in me, your love, and for being a constant in my life. Thank you to my mother-in-law, Pamela L. Foster, who saw the flowers when they were just seeds.

An extra special thank you to my beta readers: Ashley Leak, Mallory Lass, Mary Langill, James Green, Artavia Berry, David Baraza, and Bianca Samuel. Thank you for your feedback, and most importantly for sacrificing your free time to help make *Rainbow* the best book it can be.

I have an amazing editor, Kate Juniper. The universe helped me find you and I am forever grateful! Thank you to Tara Mixon who is both a phenomenal artist and book developer. I pray to work with you both for years to come!

Thank you to my wife, my sidekick, my love, Carmen-Nicole Cox. The adventures of Carmen and Sharae continue! You inspire me and push me to be my best self and I can't thank you enough. May God continue to give you the health, protection, and strength to rock with me.

Last, but certainly not least, I'd like to thank myself. I thank myself for not giving up on something I was born to do! I thank myself for seeing this crazy dream of mine through to fruition.

Shout out to Uncle Snoop for letting me know it's ok to thank myself, too! #blackqueerwritersmatter #wakandaforever